Table of Contents

Rourke Educational Media
rourkeeducationalmedia.com

Can you find these words?

Declaration

events

independence

visit

Liberty Bell

A symbol stands for an idea.

WASHINGTON
OREGON
CALIFORNIA
IDAHO
NEVADA
MONTANA
WYOMING
UTAH
ARIZONA
COLORADO
NEW MEXICO
NORTH DAKOTA
SOUTH DAKOTA
NEBRASKA
KANSAS
OKLAHOMA
TEXAS
MINNESOTA
IOWA
MISSOURI
ARKANSAS
LOUISIANA
WISCONSIN
ILLINOIS
MICHIGAN
INDIANA
OHIO
KENTUCKY
TENNESSEE
MISSISSIPPI
ALABAMA
GEORGIA
SOUTH CAROLINA
WEST VIRGINIA
VIRGINIA
PENNSYLVANIA
NEW YORK
VERMONT
NEW HAMPSHIRE
MAINE
MASSACHUSETTS
RHODE ISLAND
CONNECTICUT
NEW JERSEY
DELAWARE
MARYLAND
WASHINGTON D.C.
ALASKA
HAWAII
PACIFIC OCEAN
ATLANTIC OCEAN
PENNSYLVANIA

The Liberty Bell is in Philadelphia, Pennsylvania.

It is a symbol of freedom. It is a symbol of **independence**.

Ring, ring! The bell brought people to listen.

THE FOURTH OF JULY AT PHILADELPHIA: MR. RICHARD HENRY LEE READING THE ORIGINAL DOCUMENT OF THE DECLARATION OF INDEPENDENCE.

They heard the **Declaration** of Independence.

The Declaration brought freedom to the United States.

The bell was rung for important **events**. Now it has a crack!

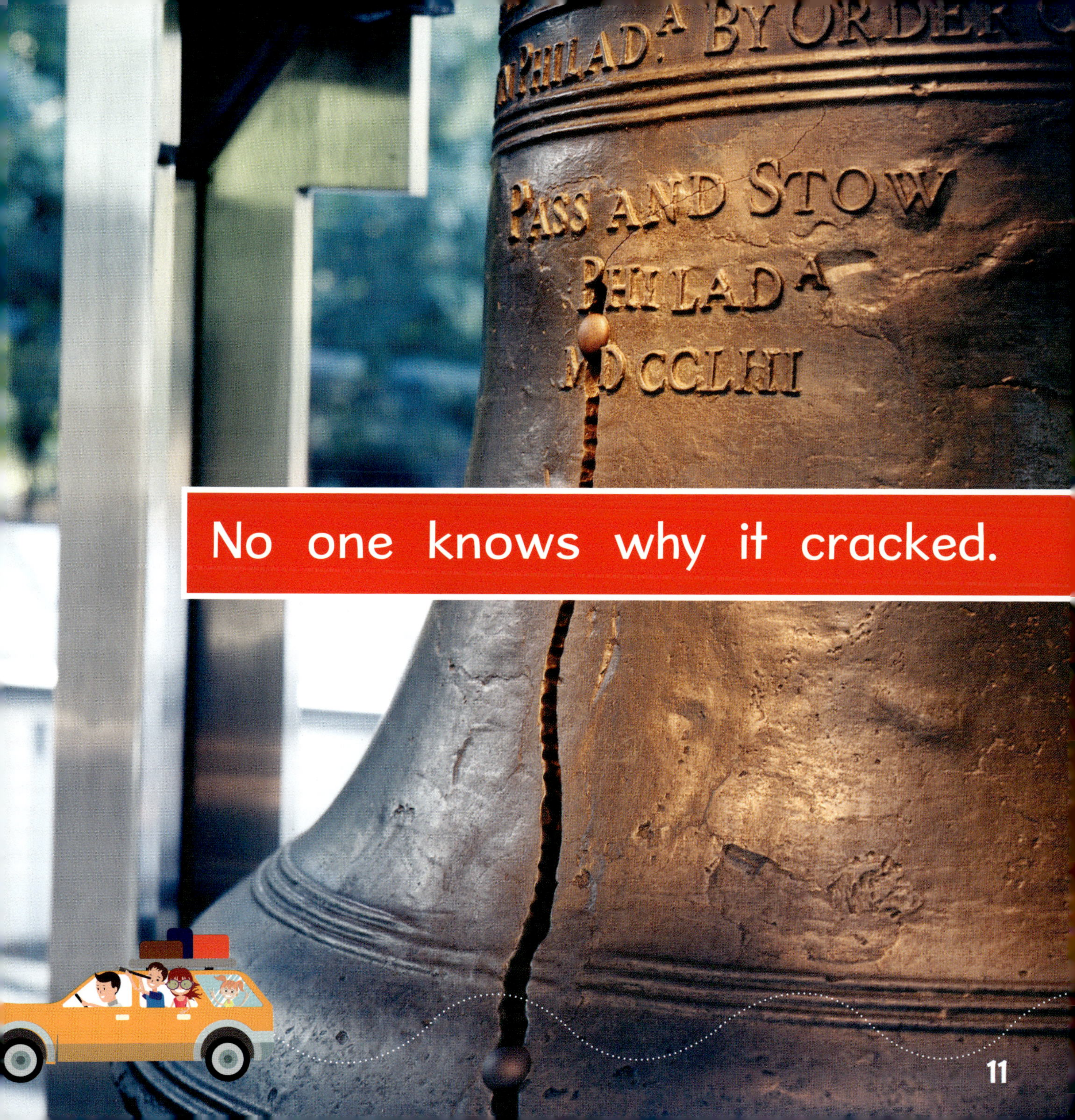

No one knows why it cracked.

The bell doesn't ring anymore. But many people **visit** it.

Did you find these words?

They heard the **Declaration** of Independence.

The bell was rung for important **events.**

It is a symbol of **independence.**

But many people **visit** it.

Photo Glossary

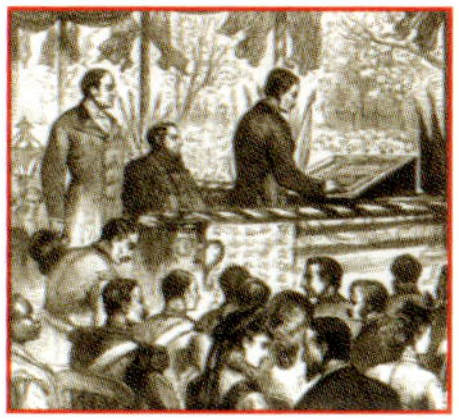

declaration (dek-luh-RAY-shuhn): An announcement of something important.

events (i-VENTS): Interesting or important activities or celebrations.

independence (in-di-PEN-duhns): Freedom, or the state of being independent.

visit (VIZ-it): To go somewhere and spend time with people or exploring a place.

Index

About the Author

K.A. Robertson is a writer and editor who enjoys learning about the history of the United States. She has visited the Liberty Bell many times!

www.rourkeeducationalmedia.com

PHOTO CREDITS: Cover: ©LoudRedCreative; p2,8,14,15: ©Library of Congress; p2,10,14,15: ©Bastiaan Slabbers; p2,6,14,15: ©Krapels; p2,13,14,15: ©Aleksander Mirski; p3: ©RomoloTavani; p4: ©f11photo; p7: ©DBTulac; p8,9: ©DNY59; p11: ©Library of Congress

Edited by: Keli Sipperley
Cover and interior design by: Kathy Walsh

Library of Congress PCN Data
Liberty Bell / K.A. Robertson
(Visiting U.S. Symbols)
ISBN 978-1-64369-059-9 (hard cover)(alk. paper)
ISBN 978-1-64369-080-3 (soft cover)
ISBN 978-1-64369-206-7 (e-Book)
Library of Congress Control Number: 2018955829

Printed in the United States of America, North Mankato, Minnesota